For Kate and Andrew
—K.R.

For Rayley and Colin
—M.S.

Clarion Books • a Houghton Mifflin Company imprint • 215 Park Avenue South, New York, NY 10003 • Text copyright © 2001 by Karen Roosa • Illustrations copyright © 2001 by Maggie Smith
The illustrations were executed in watercolor. • The text was set in 14-point Kennerley. • All rights reserved. For information about permission to reproduce selections from this book,
write to Permissions, Houghton Mifflin Company, 215 Park Avenue South, New York, NY 10003. • www.hmhco.com
Printed in China
Library of Congress Cataloging-in-Publication Data
Roosa, Karen.
Beach day / by Karen Roosa ; illustrated by Maggie Smith.   p.   cm.
Summary: Rhyming text describes a perfect day at the beach, complete with sandy knees, deviled eggs, and a castle with a moat. ISBN 0-618-02923-0
[1. Beaches—Fiction. 2. Stories in rhyme.] I. Smith, Maggie, 1965– ill. II. Title. PZ8.3.R6656 Bg 2001 [E]—dc21   00-043010

SCP   20 19 18 17 16 15 14 13
4500481466

Beach Day

by KAREN ROOSA  illustrated by MAGGIE SMITH

Clarion Books ▪ New York

Waves roar,
  Rush, and soar!
    Rolling, crashing
      To the shore.

5

Sparkling spray,
Jeweled array,
Water-skiers
On their way.

6

Sandy knees,

Foaming seas,

Insects dancing
In the breeze.

9

Noon light
Shimmers bright
In the distance,
Hot and white.

Bat, ball, mitt—
It's a hit!
Leaping, running
Lickety-split!

12

Voices chatter,

Sand pails clatter.

14

Off to lunch
The children scatter.

15

High clouds flurry,

Sand crabs scurry—

Hungry swimmers
In a hurry!

17

Chicken legs,

Deviled eggs . . .

18

What a banquet! Seagull begs.

19

Waves lapping,
Babies napping.

20

On the water
Sails are snapping.

21

Launch a boat,

Help Father float,

22

Build a castle
With a moat.

23

A freckled nose,

Sandy toes.

Ocean's salty
Sea breeze blows.

Time to pack
Picnic sack,

Bright beach towels
In a stack.

27

Late afternoon,
Supper soon.

28

Families march

Across the dune.

Sun-warmed skin,

Contented grin.

What a happy
Day it's been!